How to Surprise a DAD

by JEAN REAGAN

illustrated by LEE WILDISH

Hodder Children's Books

A division of Hachette Children's Group

for John and Jane's dad
(SURPRISE!) —J.R.

Ivy, you surprise me all the time.
Love, Dad —L.W.

First published in the United States by Alfred A. Knopf, an imprint of
Random House Children's Books, a division of Random House, Inc., New York.

This hardback edition first published in the UK in 2015 by Hodder Children's Books.

Text copyright © Jean Reagan 2015
Illustration copyright © Lee Wildish 2015

A catalogue record of this book is available from the British Library.

ISBN: 978 1 444 92466 4
10 9 8 7 6 5 4 3 2 1

Hodder Children's Books
An imprint of Hachette Children's Group
Part of Hodder & Stoughton
Carmelite House, 50 Victoria Embankment,
London EC4Y 0DZ

An Hachette UK Company
www.hachette.co.uk

Shhhhhhh!
To surprise a dad, you have to be tricky.

First of all, don't let him
see this book.

HOW TO HIDE THIS BOOK:

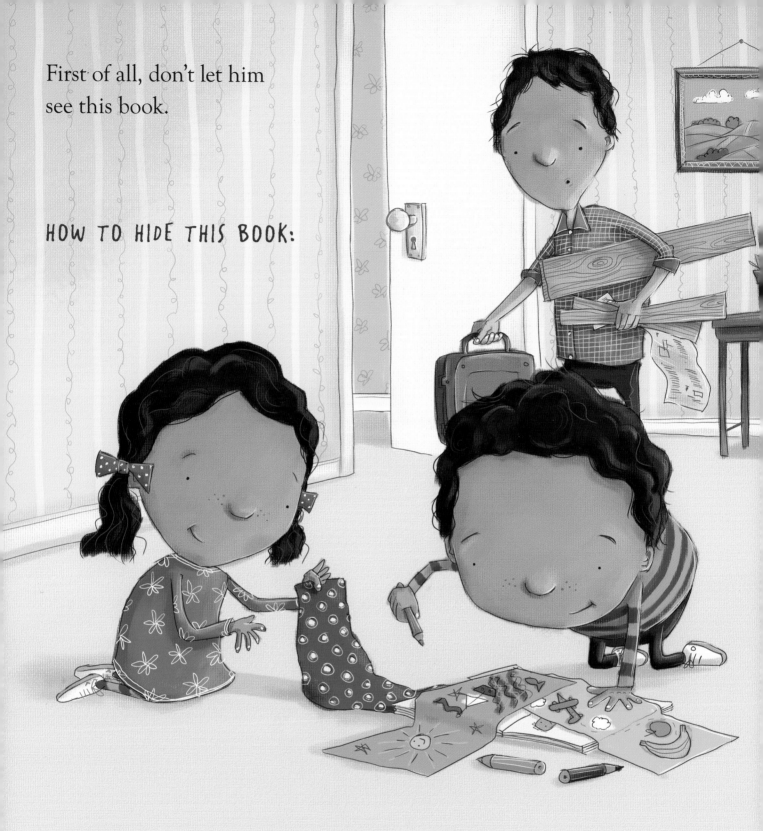

Wrap it in paper and cover it
with pictures. (That way, he'll
never know it's about him.)

Tuck it between boring books no one ever reads.

Where's the *polka-dot-hippo* book? *Wink, wink*

Make up a secret name for it, like — *polka-dot-hippo*. (Be sure to wink when you say it.)

You may already be good at surprises, but do you want
to become a *super dad-surpriser*? Great!

Luckily, *any* day is a perfect day to surprise a dad, and
there are so many different ways.

Some surprises you MAKE:

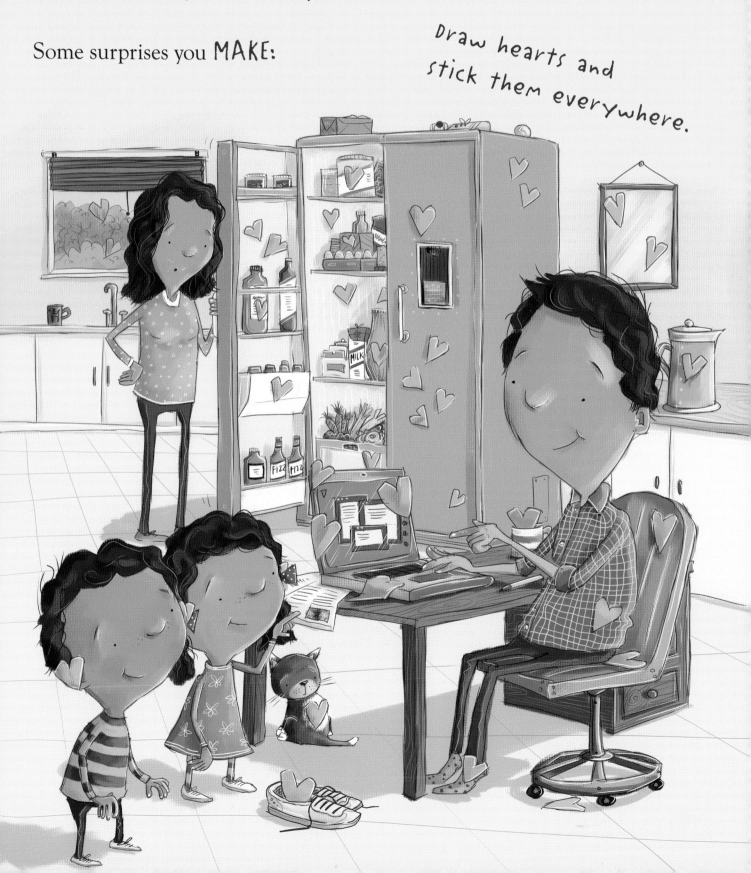

Draw hearts and
stick them everywhere.

Build a snow-dad.

Invent something amazing,
just for him.

Other surprises you **DO**:

Get his toothbrush ready.

Reorganise his shoes and hats.

Help him with the supermarket shopping.

If you want to make him laugh, walk and talk like a dad.

Some surprises you don't *make* or *do*.
Instead, you. . .

. . .FIND them.

HOW TO FIND SURPRISES:

Look up, down, under and all around.

Stay perfectly still and listen.

Dig a hole, sift through
sand or kick up leaves.

Kids have good eyes for nature (dads, not so much).
So surprise him when you find:

A caterpillar nibbling on a leaf. A squirrel hiding in a tree.
Dandelions for a bouquet. A heart-shaped rock.

A busy, busy anthill. Geese flying high above.

Now that you're an expert on *any* day surprises,
you are ready for. . . Special Day surprises!

These take a little more planning. (If your mum
is good at keeping secrets, ask her to help.)

SPECIAL DAYS FOR DADS:

His birthday

Father's Day

Congratulations

Welcome Home

CALENDAR

First, choose when to have the big surprise,
and decide who to invite:

Just your family?

Your pets? Your stuffed animals?

His Friends? Your Friends?

Relatives? Neighbours?

Then, decorate with his favourite colour. Keep it simple or
go wild! (Remember to save some ideas for next time.)

Now, plan the yummiest part of the surprise – THE TREATS!

Create a dessert that looks like your dad.
Bake cookies with extra chocolate chips.

It's your dad's special day, so be sure to have his favourites:

Spicy crisps
Smoked oysters
Super-stinky cheese

Don't forget presents!

PRESENTS FOR A DAD:

Shirt and tie.
(Instead of wrapping these,
wear them for an even
bigger surprise.)

Everything you need
to make paper aeroplanes
together.

A secret treasure
map of your garden.

Coupons!

(Check also: ANY DAY SURPRISES you make, do or find.)

If your dad gets suspicious and asks,

Look innocent.
(Practise this in a mirror.)

Say something like, "It's very boring
behind you. You shouldn't turn around."

Think fast — distract him with
a crazy dance!

When it's surprise time, make sure everyone is hiding.

HOW TO HIDE EVERYONE:

Between the pictures,
plants or balloons.

Surprise!

Behind the curtains,
sofa or coat rack.

Under the table, cushions
or blankets.

While you wait for your dad, practise whispering "Surprise."

OK, now shhhhhhhh. . .

Remember, of *all* the surprises, the best ones are
the special ones you dream up just for *your* dad.

Now, don't forget to hide this book. And *shhhhhhh!*

If you *do* want to let your dad read it,
have him say this pledge aloud
before he starts:

I, Dad,
promise not to remember
anything in this book.
Especially anything about surprises.

I ♥ DAD

FOR DAD'S FAVOURITE COOKIES
- flour
- chocolate
- eggs
- butter
- more chocolate
- sprinkles

ONE CLEAN ROOM COUPON.

Presents for DAD
- Drill
- Ball
- Hat and Scarf
- Hair gel
- Play day

LEAF FOR DAD

DAD + MUM = ME

TOP-SECRET!